What lies at the end of the rainbow? Is there merely a pot of gold, or might there be another sort of treasure — a treasure that may be reached by anyone willing to undertake the journey?

For if you follow the rainbow to its end and look into its shimmering colors, you will find a great oak tree with a door at the base of the trunk.

If you open the door and step inside, you will meet Mrs. Murgatroyd™, the wise woman who lives there. In her paint pots she collects all the colors of the rainbow.

And if you take up a paintbrush and picture whatever is in your heart, you will discover a treasure far more valuable than gold.

# And Peter Said Goodbye

Series concept by Ayman Sawaf and Kevin Ryerson
Developed from actual case histories by art therapist Liz Farrington
Copyright ©1993 by Enchanté Publishing
MRS. MURGATROYD character copyright ©1993 by Enchanté
MRS. MURGATROYD is a trademark of Enchanté
Series format and design by Jaclyne Scardova
Edited by Gudrun Höy. Story editing by Bobi Martin

Enchanté Publishing
P.O. Box 620471, Woodside, CA 94062

Printed in Singapore

Library of Congress Cataloging-in-Publication Data
Farrington, Liz.
And Peter said goodbye/story created by Liz Farrington,
written by Jennifer C. Weil; illustrated by Jaclyne Scardova. — 2nd ed.
        p.      cm.
Summary: Mrs. Murgatroyd's magical paints send Peter on a journey across
the country to his grandfather's funeral and help him cope with his feelings
of grief and loss.
ISBN 1-56844-100-2
[1. Death - Fiction. 2. Grandfathers - Fiction]   I. Weil, Jennifer C.
II. Scardova, Jaclyne, ill.  III. Title.
PZF.F24618An      1995         (Fic.)—dc20        95-36443

Second Edition
10  9  8  7  6  5  4  3  2  1

# And Peter Said Goodbye

Story created by Liz Farrington
Written by Jennifer C. Weil
Illustrated by Jaclyne Scardova

Enchanté Publishing

Peter stared at his blank notebook. How could he write about "Life in Connecticut" when Grandpa was dead? Fresh tears slipped down his cheeks. Quickly wiping them away, Peter looked around at the rest of his class. Everyone was busy writing, except his best friend. Lee smiled but Peter quickly looked back at his paper. He was tired and his head ached. When the last bell rang, he grabbed his books and rushed out the door.

"Hey, Peter! Wait up," Lee called behind him, but Peter pretended not to hear and ran toward home.

Changing his mind, Peter cut through the field and headed for Wick Creek. He stopped at a special spot. Peter remembered the time he and Grandpa had caught a two-pound bass here and the time Grandpa had hooked a slimy, old, cotton hat. Grandma washed it and Grandpa always wore it fishing after that.

Once they'd built a cubbyhole out of some rocks to keep their lunch cool. Now Peter shoved his books in the hole and sat under their favorite tree. He felt close to Grandpa here.

Peter knew he couldn't stay long. His neighbor, Mrs. Palachek, would be coming by to fix supper and stay with him while his parents were in California for Grandpa's funeral.

"Why can't I go to the funeral, too?" he'd asked his parents.

His father momentarily paused and said, "We don't want you to miss school, son."

"But I want to see Grandpa," he'd insisted.

"Peter, honey, you don't understand," his mother had said.

"You don't understand!" Peter shouted back.

Jumping up, he picked up a stone and hurled it at the water.
"Nobody understands!" Peter threw another stone.
The splash of the water made a beautiful rainbow that
shimmered toward the sky.

Looking up, Peter saw a woman holding pots of paint.
Little rainbows seemed to be flowing into the pots.

"Hello, Peter. How nice that you've come," she said.

"How do you know my name?" Peter asked.

"I know the names of all the children who need me." She smiled at him.

"I'm Mrs. Murgatroyd. May I show you something?"

Peter nodded. Mrs. Murgatroyd went to a nearby oak tree.

"This is where I keep my magical rainbow paints." She reached out and opened a door in the tree. "Do you like painting?"

"Yes," Peter said.

"The rainbows give magic to the paints," said Mrs. Murgatroyd. "Paint whatever you wish and let the magical paints help you, Peter."

Peter thought a moment, then picked up a brush and began to paint. When he was done he showed his picture to Mrs. Murgatroyd. "This is my robot. He has rooms inside and lots of windows. He can take me anywhere I want to go!"

A sudden gust of wind whisked Peter's picture out the door.

"Run after it, Peter," said Mrs. Murgatroyd.

Peter bounded after the painting, but when he picked it up, the paper was blank!

"Here I am, Peter," boomed a deep voice.

Peter was surprised to find himself staring up at the giant robot he had just painted!

"Hop in," said the robot.

Peter looked at Mrs. Murgatroyd. "Go ahead," she said.
"You painted him, and you told me he could take you anywhere."

Peter opened the door he'd painted on the robot's ankle.
The inside was just the way he'd imagined it!

"Wow!" said Peter. "If Grandpa could see this!"
That gave him an idea. "Robot, take me to California!"

"Okay, Peter," boomed the robot. He began to jog across the countryside as if it were a toy set. Peter watched through a window in the robot's neck. In no time at all, they were in California.

Suddenly a thick fog seemed to surround them. Looking down, Peter spotted his grandfather crossing the street. Grandpa didn't see the car speeding toward him in the fog.

"Look out, Grandpa!" Peter screamed.

Brake lights glowed pink through the fog. The car swerved but couldn't avoid hitting Grandpa. "No!" Peter cried. "Don't be dead, Grandpa!"

But Peter knew it was true. His father had told him about the accident.

Turning from the window, Peter grabbed one of the pillows from the bed and punched it as hard as he could. "Stupid driver!" he yelled. "I hate you! And I hate fog!" Flinging himself onto the bed, he pounded the mattress with his fists.

"I shouldn't have let you move to California! Why weren't you more careful, Grandpa?"

Peter sobbed with frustration and rage until he was exhausted, then he fell asleep.

He dreamed his parents had taken him to the funeral. Beautiful flowers filled the room. *Grandpa would have liked these flowers,* Peter thought.

When the service was over, Peter saw people walk by the coffin. Some placed a flower there. Peter chose a rose, Grandpa's favorite flower. As he laid it on the coffin, the petals became rainbow colored.

"Goodbye, Grandpa," he whispered. "I'll love you forever."

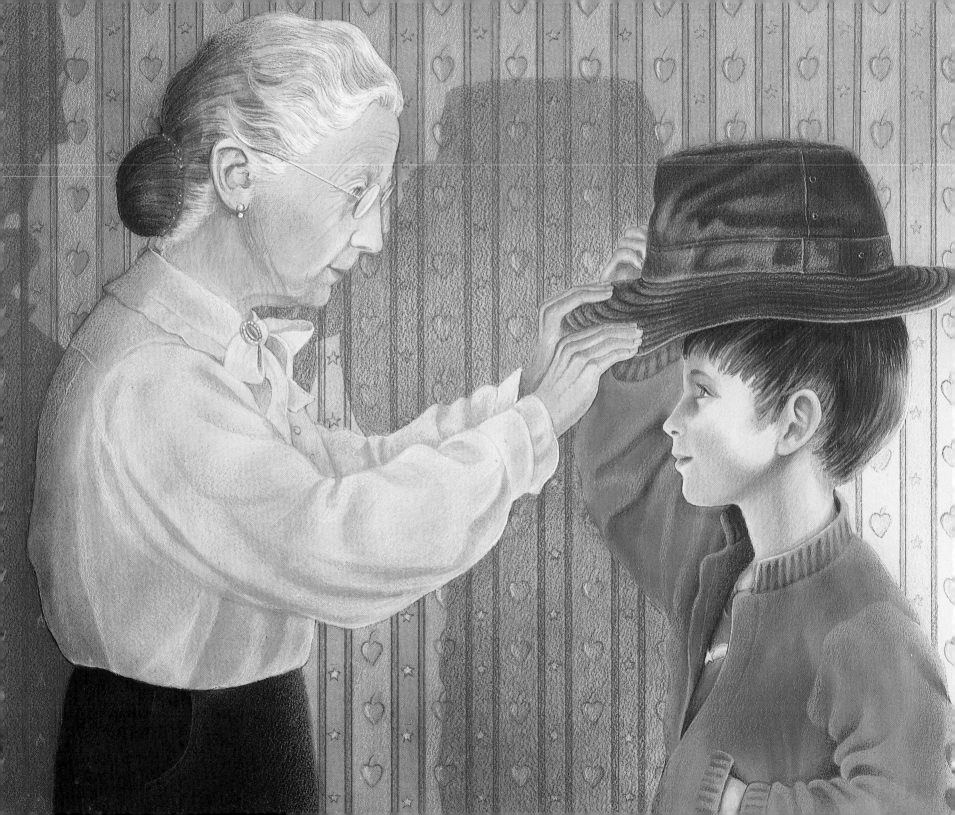

Later, everyone gathered at his grandparents' house.
People began to talk about things they had done with Grandpa.

"Hey, Dad, remember the time Grandpa thought he had a big fish,
and it turned out to be an old hat?" Peter asked.

"That reminds me," said Grandma. "Come with me a moment, Peter."
They went into another room and Grandma found the fishing hat.
"I'd like you to have this," she said. "It will help you remember Grandpa.
In a way, he'll always be with us in our memories."

Peter still felt sad. Then he remembered what Mrs. Murgatroyd had said. *"Let the magic paints help you."*

*Grandpa liked parties with music and dancing*, he thought. *He wouldn't want us all to be sad.*

Smiling, Peter painted a picture where all the people wore brightly colored clothing. Rainbows and music were everywhere.

*I can paint pictures of good times I remember sharing with Grandpa,* thought Peter. He smiled remembering last Christmas when they decorated the tree. Grandpa had played Christmas carols on his banjo while Grandma made hot cocoa with whipped cream on top.

He remembered a spring day when Grandpa had taken him out in the meadow. They had watched birds making nests, picked some wildflowers for Grandma, and surprised a rabbit.

A sudden noise awakened Peter. At first he was startled to find himself under a tree near the creek. *Why was it so dark?* Then he remembered his dream. Peter shivered from the cold. His stomach growled. *Oh no! Mrs. Palachek!* Quickly, he grabbed his books from the cubbyhole and raced for home. *I hope Mrs. Palachek isn't too mad,* he thought.

As Peter ran into his yard, he was surprised to see his parents' car. "Mom! Dad!" he hollered as he bounded up the steps. His parents rushed out to meet him.

"Peter! We were so worried about you," his mother said as she gave him a big hug.

"I went to the creek to think about Grandpa," Peter said, "and I guess I fell asleep."

"Grandma wanted you to have Grandpa's fishing hat," said Dad. Peter smiled and said, "I know."

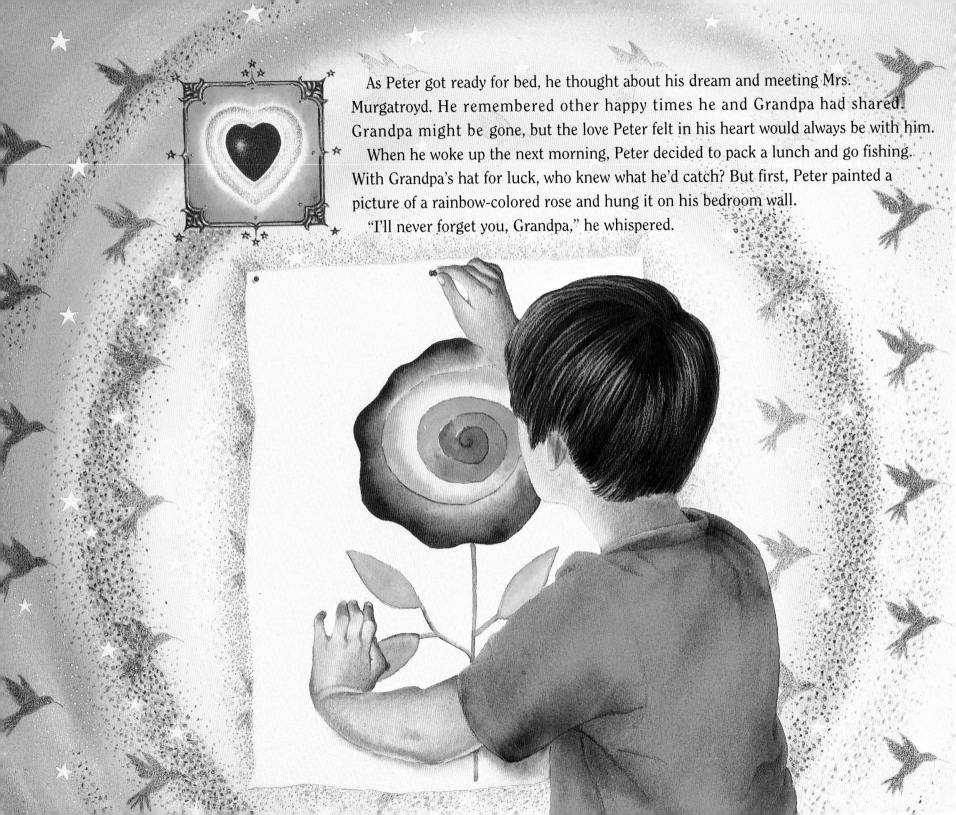

As Peter got ready for bed, he thought about his dream and meeting Mrs. Murgatroyd. He remembered other happy times he and Grandpa had shared. Grandpa might be gone, but the love Peter felt in his heart would always be with him.

When he woke up the next morning, Peter decided to pack a lunch and go fishing. With Grandpa's hat for luck, who knew what he'd catch? But first, Peter painted a picture of a rainbow-colored rose and hung it on his bedroom wall.

"I'll never forget you, Grandpa," he whispered.

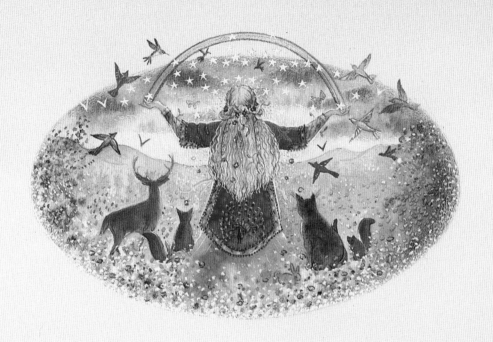